PRIMER OF THE OBSOLETE

PRIMER OF THE OBSOLETE
Diane Glancy

UNIVERSITY OF MASSACHUSETTS PRESS

Amherst and Boston

Copyright © 2004 by University of Massachusetts Press
All rights reserved
Printed in the United States of America

LC 2003027675
ISBN 1-55849-444-8

Designed by Sally Nichols
Set in Perpetua
Printed and bound by Sheridan Books, Inc.

Library of Congress Cataloging-in-Publication Data

Glancy, Diane.
    Primer of the obsolete / Diane Glancy.
        p. cm.
    "Winner of the 2003 Juniper Prize for Poetry."
    ISBN 1-55849-444-8 (pbk. : alk. paper)
    1. Indians of North America—Poetry.   2. Racially mixed
    people—Fiction.   3. Multiculturalism—Poetry.   I. Title.
    PS3557.L294P75 2004
    811'.54—dc22   2003027675

British Library Cataloguing in Publication data are available.

For Orvezene Lewis Hall, my grandmother,
for Lewis Hall, my father,
and for those voices we heard on the road to her place,
and on the open road to other places when he was no longer with me.
For the meandering road of language that will let you do a lot of things
to it before it protests. For the Savior and the pinings in the backwoods
apostolic churches. For Rooty, the mah-un, wherever he is.
This is for all of you.

ACKNOWLEDGMENTS

Grateful acknowledgment is made to the editors of the following publications in which these poems first appeared:

The Alembic for "Sketchy Goings"; *American Writing: A Magazine* for "American Aboriginal"; *Five Fingers Review* for "I Have a Fever Blister Mister I Might Have Got from You"; *Furnitures: The Magazine of North American Ideophonics* for "Lord of the Stable Lord of the Rack," "A Trailer That Follows Back" and "I Have My Hand on the Gearshift of My Space Ship and on the Horn"; *Harrisburg Review* for "Puff & Toot"; *The Iowa Review* for "The Buffalo at No Wait Cafe," "Caint Aint Abel," "*Blue House with People*," and "Generalist Custer My Highway Man My Trucker"; *Lake Region Review* for "Why I Like God" and "The Aviatrix at Russell Doughtery School"; *New Zoo Review* for "For Stephanie"; *RACS / Rent a Chicken Speaks* for "Crows"; *The Raven Chronicles* for "8 Ball"; *Xcp Cross Cultural Poetics* for "Velcro," "Tongues," and "I am your true woman, Blinky"; The Poetry Project, St. Mark's Church, New York City, for electronic publication on their website of "NOah's arK," "Leeroy's Wife Paint Nails," "Primer of the Obsolete," and "Ranger Otto Ranger Clive"; *bite to eat place: an anthology of contemporary food poetry and poetic prose*, edited by Anne F. Walker and Andrea Adolph (Baton Rouge, La.: Redwood Coast Press, 1995), for "Generally he gave them plenty of room"; and *Sister Nations: Native American Women Writers on Community*, edited by Heid E. Erdrich and Laura Tohe (St. Paul: Minnesota Historical Society Press, 2002), for "The Great Spirit's Wife" and "The Abandoned Wife Gives Herself to the Lord."

Thanks also to Chax Press, Tucson, Arizona, for first publishing a few poems from *Primer of the Obsolete* as a chapbook.

Prefatory Note

Several years ago, I saw an exhibit called *Passionate Visions of the American South: Self-Taught Artists from 1940 to the Present*, a collection of folk art using house paint, model airplane paint, tar on scrap metal, cardboard, tin, and whatever could be found. I wanted to go back and retrieve the primitiveness that was in my family. The roughness. The texture of the old voices. How do you relate the native to America? Pick up what was left after the continental divide of language. Learn to tango with a partner not your own, who is not doing what you think the tango is anyway. I wanted to use the thought patterns and rhythms from the mix of the worlds I have experienced. Put them together in a new way. The Cherokee and white. Old conjurers of tribal magic and circuit preachers. The connection also to the black culture before the removal trail to Indian territory. Then the cavalry. The intermix of Christianity. The short bursts of the Bible from the telegraph wire. Those spirits I hear still running on the roof.

Go:-li ni-ga-l'-s-ti-(ya) (ha)
Sv-hi-ye ni-ga-l'-s-ti-(ya') (ha')
Ko:ga-(a) (i) u-g'-ta a-gi(?) -a

from the Cherokee

They have been there a long time,
rolling their r's, and waiting.

Larry Levis, "A Study of Three Crows"
from *The Dollmaker's Ghost*

I look at his books
and see the little words
and think perhaps they are functional.

Carolyn Erler

Contents

PRIMER OF THE OBSOLETE

The Buffalo at No Wait Cafe

Here I am a little buffalo wiping tables with my tail. It was the only
job I could get what with my size. They killed so many of us.
_____ million. Sometimes soldiers shot from trains passing.
We didn't have sense to know what was happening. It was called
extermination a word lovely as crematorium you'd think was in the
butterworks.

It wasn't his fault he couldn't hear the right man who said *don't go darling don't*. He could have if his ears opened heart stopped at the sight of the Cheyenne and Dakota the spirit-warriors and whoever else joined. A troop of them trucking out west. The lonesome cowboy there on the hill.

The Abandoned Wife Gives Herself to the Lord

My heart is warm like fire, but there are cold spots
in it. I don't know how to talk. I want to be a white man.
My Father did not tell me it was wrong to
have so many wives. I love all my women. My old
wife is a mother to the others; I can't do without her,
but she is old and cannot work very much; I can't
send her away to die. This woman cost me ten
horses; she is young; she will take care of me when
I am old. I want to do right. I'm not a bad man.
I know your new law is good.

Chief Mark considers monogamy at the Warm Springs Agency, 1871

She felt dizzy with hunger. The spirits began to speak. She saw
the Holy One on his cloud spearing something. He fished as if he
had a claw and the salmon jumped to him. She sat on the rock
waiting for him to see her. She'd heard his believers called the
Bride of Christ. She knew he was a man who took more than one
wife.

LORD OF THE STABLE LORD OF THE RACK

I'm coming loveliest cowpoke
my lariat over my saddle horn
a frypan for those trail pancakes at first light
my chaps and blanket
saddle bag
bedroll
my hoof pick
horse-tail wrap
mane tamer
my hobbles in my hand.

CAINT AINT ABEL
pastel on brown paper bag

However God made thingks knowd He made knowd He wanted
Blood which Abel brought in the Tupperware of his hands from the
Lamb he kilt and God said right Abel. But to Caint He sait no your
harvest aint what I want but the Blood which is the foreshadow of
Christ. If I can speak honestly with You God as Instructor of this
writing class a little hard to take I mean You know Your subtext
is not always clear. If you want an A on Your structure You can't
have sudden turns you know but plotted for. But You won't
do nothingt but have it Your own way. You're uncompromising
if I can say so though You say it isn't Your fault just like no
brother's keeper.

I Have a Fever Blister Mister I Might Have Got from You

Looking in a store window and you could choose
if you had the cash
or how you say what you say is the point
in this bifactual age
the close-up language of new delights
conversely
how Jesus referred to himself
in the form of another
manna forinstance that rained in the wilderness
notwithstanding a drought.

MODEL AIRPLANE PAINT ON CORRUGATED SCRAP METAL

It was a saint of a night the darkness a single man who knowd something of heaven as a story of his own view. Of all the skies it was the one drawd by the night over him he wrote. His rake caught the stars. The eucalyptus leaves curled on the yard like quarter moons.

SKETCHY GOINGS

I am warm. I have seen fire.
Isaiah 33:16

There was Abraham, his toy son, Isaac, in the space behind the
dollhouse stairs. Maybe a tiny desert on a table. A mountain
maybe on it. The back of the house open to give them room.
Upstairs, Sarah, the dollhouse mother, reading a story to her girl.

> *She had twigs for toes she fingered little*
> *holes in the ground she made a scaffolding*
> *of branches with her voice she made a fire.*

The dollhouse daughter listening with a placid look on her face as
if she had openings in her head.

THE LORD RAINS

You know Him by His verbs

His wife's story to God states
now there's only water on his hands
ain't nobody here long enough
before he knowd he wasn't meant
to houseboat over the choppy little beasts of waves
he hears them gnaw the boat like squirrels
the dampness of everythingk
couldn't have been longer
there's mildew on the pages of the words I write
he sweeps the county where we land
shoos the yellowtails
spoonbills
scissortails.

BRIDE OF CHRIST

I will bring the blind by a way they knew not; I will
lead them in paths they have not known. I will
make the darkness light before them and crooked
things straight. These thing will I do unto them, and
not forsake . . .

Isaiah 42:16

Now that I was I didn't knowd the anger of the dark but was
brought out as a pure bride from her house for the Husband of
Light. Oh yo the wedding stories them chroniclers made their
tongues to cover. He knowd us by our praise. He's blind maybe of
His own Light, but hears our sound, His one element drawd by the
other. We hear His walking stick tapping the walk to find the curb.
Those soldiers marched us on a trail. They kilt the buffalo for their
tongues, left the carcasses floating above the prairie without a way to
form their words how could they rise?

Doot Dah Do

Once the earth was new
and the animals still shiny,
the cellophane hardly off them,
the tags still stuck on.
They squeaked funny new sounds.
And man was new, still wet in places.
He named the animals,
said *lets do already lets*.
So they did their dooed and died
and the Great Spirit sorrowed over the dooed
they did.
He created them so He could talk to someone,
you know how it is to be the Great Spirit,
if you've ever been disappointed and alone,
that's what it's like.
Only He has the power, of course,
to make things talk,
the power to shut them up,
the power you know to make the rain.
Then afterwards men were new again,
the animals by two this time,
but men still said *lets do*
and did their dooed and died again.
So the Great Spirit said *nuf*.
He made Chief Jesus to died for them
so they would not forever
in their died state dooed.
But they sent Him back with holes in His hands
from their campsite which dogs guard and bit.
They said, *let's dooed* and still they did,
but others saw the bite holes
and became new dooders
and plugged him in and stopped
dunning the dooed they did.

11

The Translation Mobile

Let me drive the moving van
when we fly to heaven.
Not a Mayflower
no, one of them *wuz e'nuf*.
But a translation mobile.
See them pearlie gates
through the storm clouds over west.
I want to shift those gears
without a hitch
an 18 wheeler with a rudder for crossing Jordan
a satalite dish
mobile phone
rocket booster
a map for the galaxy
Aaron Neville singing *Ave Maria*
for the trucks lined up at that weight station
there.

Puff & Toot

There in the hereafter. Above the farbelow. Puffed up & tooted. Tooted up & puffed. The characters are the main bones. There's no threading them together. They fall at every step. They land on every throne. Crowd 'em in thereafter. Get door closed. Lord move over. It tight in the wherehere.

No One Has to Cross Jordan Alone
Howard Finster
enamel on tin mirror

HEAVEN IS THE END OF FAITH
HEAVEN IS THE END OF TEMPTATION
HEAVEN IS THE END OF DEATH
HEAVEN IS THE END OF PRAYER
HEAVEN IS THE END OF HUNGRY

All them Bannerisms floating Skyward with the Loaf of Heaven.
Look at Jesus upright on the waves. The white lights zinging from
him like rifle-fire. Anybody else would sink. His feet must be the
visible waves on which He walks. The white dressed Angels *robe-
ing* above Jesus waiting. Their faces, arms, their little wingings,
their lifting grace, flapping like gnats all over God's sky, *speeding*
Him upward. Jesus looking toward them. His face dry as
campfire. His hands cleanly raised as if He'd just washed them.
Yoppo. *That White Cloud Thing* behind Him must be an Idea of
Heaven above the water. Hallelujah, we're crossing the Jordan,
Father God, Jubliant Host, we're joining the edge. Reach us as we
reach.

BIRDFOOD

Unlike the others
he marched us forward to make more room
I mean not for that reason
but because He liked us
let us into His house
let us fall
gave us room to get up from mistakes
and stumble again all over the place.

NOah's arK

Touissaint Auguste, Haitian, b. 1925
Seattle Art Museum

God's for the ark's small flocks and herds . . .
They are here . . . in the marble air . . .
Miraculously aloft
above that flood and flaw
Where Noah darkly plies his craft.

"Rara Avis in Terris," Anthony Hecht

He must have prayed the rain god, *shut it up.*
Must have prayed the oars would hold.
No, there waz no oaring but an arK-on-water-tagging.
Dere waz no outboard, sail. Faceit.
Dey wadn't going nowhere hop-sacked in a gunny-race.

The fish *underarked, un course,*
spared an acquarium onboard
but gave the fish OVER the 2 x 2 of animal, fowl.
What close-call decision to leave the turtle on board?
Dat platypus, well?

One son in overalls whisperin' to taper.
Stand still, he say. You goin'.
Get in line w/ turkey, donkey, burro, goat, camel,
sheep, swan, monkey, chicken, insect, buffalo.

The daughters-in-law carryun' covered dish
da shape of cow. Dey carry rabbit pitcher, cayenne,
calabash, scrabble board, arkabilia.
The fleables of 2 worlds confluing.

Had he tied yet seal, the sea lion behind the arK?

16

Which here dis a barge painted red
w/ thatch-roof cabin.

The amputated trees *doomified.*

Rear-ended by the rain, *dey didn't know howlong*
the barge would gloat w/neighs, howls, da buzzings
of the four legged, the winged, the creeping.
The *jesup jesup of da lick.*
But a barge is a barge.
We are pastured after this.
Oourear drum's all that's left of floating.

He must have called, just a *little land*
from his ham radio.
Stayable those long nights they played words:
eardquake, volcano, blizurd, poler bear, mukuluk.
Such noise the nocturnals couldn't open their eyes,
groogy from lack of day-sleep with all the floatful
sloshing.

Dey must ha' neoned under marquee lightning.
Da scrabble letteers spellun' hammer, anvul, stur'up.
The curvature of the ear's loading ramp.
The hippopotamuses, *zooed.* The loons, bees, the *bozings.*

Did Noah, say, *open windo get some air*
in dis parking lot?
The animales trying to get their balancind act,
the scrabbleboard listing.
God from arK: iz it what we aR we hear?
or maybe rain on the roof kept the animals *dozey,*
or the oscillating *fan hummin' w/dem askin'*
why dey buy ticket
for this floating life *dis cruize.*

17

A Wife

She was in a little apron covering her like a hand.
She kept saying at the stove
it was not bread eating her alone.
Sometimes she felt waves pasting from the back.
Sometimes she felt another woman standing at the stove.
You could almost hear her voice.
She didn't have an apron.
She didn't know if she was supposed to act older
to politely say how lovely
even though she couldn't see

but she knew how
to say things she didn't mean _____.

May God cook upon her with kindness.

In my dream there was a house moving

Its kitchen yellow
the large oak sawed off at the ground
because it had grown into the wall of the house
and could not be separate
but how to get from here to there
my mother's lesson
I would always know a house that moved
because of the tree with birds in its leaves
where there was a child
I could pick up and hold out of the desolation
but the saddness maybe not
even though God was in the air.

Why I Like God

stay out late He says
do whatever you want
wear My shield and helmet anytime
nothing will get you
not even those *squeaky* nights
fly between the surfboards of My wings
say *I come from a pit I stand on a rock*
pike a torpedo into the sky
light as a sharp trombone
paste the metal body of My plane
you can fly to My yard
dry when you land
sometimes clear
sometimes abundant with wind-changed
flocks of sheep
their shifting migrations over the earth
are shapes you can fly through
if you want
straight to the sliver of the moon
crawling through the sky on its hands and toes.

I Have My Hand on the Gearshift of My Space Ship and on the Horn

Rooty be my *mah-un*
fly with me to the blue space in the ship that leaks to the sphere
you know flying through us we never know until we wake and eat
our cornflakes the light of gravity diminishing like the hope we
would ever come back from here.

SWEATLODGE

He saw some rocks for the sweatlodge by the road nearly put me
through the windshield to stop. The rocks give their lives. You
see the orange sparks. The voices of the rocks when they're carried
from the fire into the pit of the lodge. The offering of sage. The
dipper of water splashing the rocks like a steam engine trying to
rise before a trip. The chuckle of the thought. You hear your own
voice saying, *Great Spirit Give Me Patience Strength Lord Help
Me Get Through This.*

So the said treaties

The said Indians may have and enjoy theire
wanted conveniences of Oystering, fishing, and
gathering Tuccahoe, Curtenemmons, wild oats,
rushes, Puckonne or anything else theire natural
Support not usefull to the English. That no
fforreigne Indian be suffered to come to any
Englishman's plantacon without a friendly
Neighbor Indian in his Company.

1677 Powhatan Treaty with the
Governor of Virginia

There's the joy of being conjoined
to the retreatable language
the reverence of words changing (hop soc)
the *newbrains* of revisions.
We saw their syntax from the distance
their words industrialized
tool and dye casted.
We woke to them shortening their stories to blurps.
The hoped space we had in their words sack-raced the lawn.
A chest of drawers
the beds over which their continuums beat
the large net of keeping us from landing.
It was more work than alone
to stay out of their way
their discordancies shoving us until the room.

The Last Supper

W. Hawkins, 1895–1990, Kentucky
enamel and cornmeal on plywood

A plop of grease in the frypan
a little batter
the Indian coming several actually who wanted cornbread
still warm on the plate the steam like a tongue
they had some trip to make upriver
the stink of grease on everything
like the aftersmell of smoke from the cookstove
the hour of the day curling.

Bill Traylor
colored pencil on cardboard
(Or, *Jum kicking the roof*)

You watch the step of someone on the roof you could desize with
your words but you climb the new truth of *infictive*. You see the
blue screen of the sky. The drive-in movie. The spirit car-hops.
The *goings*. It was a pure step to ask the birds to spread their
wings for a tablecloth as if it were a holy ghost meeting and the Lord
dressed as a stork with dolls gave the birds your crumbs
saying *birdie birdie megwetch for your wings*.

IRREDENTA

If you want to take the country back don't you think that's going too far? I mean the Aboriginals wanted Sydney can you imagine people moving back across the water saying yes take it all? The banks the buildings the opera house like a sail boat on the water. Or we'll uproot the buildings if the Aboriginals want. The pipes and wires dangling from the planes as we leave.

The Audubon Society sells seed in winter. Niger thistle, cracked corn, millet, sunflower, manna suet cakes, for whatever flies. Finches, quail, crows. The men talk about Indians who used to drive to Pawhuska and walk up Main Street, horns and buffalo robes on the hood of their cars. Sometimes running out of gas, they walked away and left them there. *Generally he gave them plenty of room*, he says. They wrapped in blankets in those days wore moccasins and feathers. A sack of seed would feed the Cherokee when old and sick they a) flew, b) begged, c) _____ like birds.

Velcro

The fields open the skie if crops don't come the topsoil blows them
away. The Dust Bowl wift the durt liftd skiewurd. We gave it all
away. The durt-mounds bie the Missouri River in Iowa are fields
frum Oklahoma lifted. We drive thair in trucks to get ddurt back.
Shuvel all night. How many truckloady you think dis take?
Thair're windbreaks now between fields to keep durdt back. We
knowd our story but no one telling. This ropad we drivin a
history shuffled into remembering differently than it was hurd.

A Trailer That Follows Back

Sometimes words move. You can't always find them when you come back. Maybe they turned migratory. You follow them with the tongue of history in your mouth. At night the deer step out of their arms. The words don't know what to do. Sometimes they can't hear. The roots of beans and corn in the fields. The bears in the caves of their ears.

IF THEN PEOPLE WALKED (OR BOATED)

> Cherokees relinquish to the United States
> all their lands east of the Mississippi.
>
> Treaty with the Cherokee, 1835

Where were they walking
what from? how many
miles _____
if then there were people walking
what were they walking to for?
where to?
travel not of choice
but force
not so much wanting to go but having
resigned somewhat yet regretting the lack
of not much say in the matter
so they went
how many waves _____ of them
the other world there to get them
if they didn't make it
the one hanging over them like an oar
not untoward as they said
but endeavoring to make the effort
they walked
it was solemn as daylight
in getting so far from wanting
they could in fact
rev up
to step (or row) that border
across.

IF I'M NOT ON THE ROAD I DON'T THINK I'M GETTING ANYWHERE (OR) HOC SIC)

What with weather overhead
the wounded

don't they know
history is overwith

well pick up
go on

get that child
(hurt)

out of the way
say all right

you've cried
now get on.

BAKEY

. . . of making many treaties there is no end
Ecclesiastes 12:12

Don't they listen to nothing but their own?
I'm getting tired I am
of this wandering through
the stalks of *exenergies*
all thumped up
reverences all newted out
invariably more than one could *ink*
from the tedious *gump* of stuff
how do they go on?

LEEROY'S WIFE PAINT NAILS

Now there are ten of them.

As I Lay Dying
William Faulkner

She paint the nail like a boat she rowd.
She leave polish in the wake of her rowing.
She couldn't cross the ice midwinter
but whad's the fingernail but a frozen surface?
Dis thumb a pontoon she say to customer
who stomp out'ta place.
Leeroy's wife think bloodhounds after her.
She shellack floors of 5 rooms in 2 houses.
She paint the nail pale as freezer burn
or fishbucket under surface of Tenkiller where fish swim.
She paint 10 windows w/ shade pull down.
She rowd 5 continents 5 oceans.
She paint Leeroy taillights leavin on the road.
Sometimes she paint rakd mapleleafs.
She set fire to field with foxtail Samson tied to torch.
She think Jesus while she work.
She paint the bloodholes in His hands.
His knuckles like beavermounds when His fingers bend.
When she find stone roll from tomb
she paint the nails of risen
Holy Christ.

If she could have one thing it would be a clapper she said. You
hit your hands and the light goes off. She wanted that when she went
to bed at night or just sat in the room clapping a lightning storm onto
the horizon in a dry spell. She could dream in darkness yet if she
wanted to see the spirits over her bed at night she could clap her
hands and watch them roll like a tornado up the backroad something
like the tongue in the Great Spirit's mouth.

AIR

Beloved plane flying the 4-cornered sky. What're you doing in the sky pinked with our prayers? *Hey you plane*! we call to the *buzwan* sky, but you pass without listening, drumming your aloneness once you've surmised the loose air in your *up-there* flight.

She buries her face in the paper as if looking with the navigator at a chart. Her voice thin as a vapor trail above the air. I can't hear and I stand next to her. Does she expect the class to listen to the distance she offers? While heat-ducts whirrr like a twin-engine plane. Maybe the *Electra's* in flight again. I want to burst from the room but I'm a captive of the small voice. The aviatrix's deadly as a monsoon. She stumbles over the words until the bell rings. She offers empty boxes above the storage cabinet. A mouth the size of some remote island. A voice failing on the wireless over the ocean somewhere.

FOR STEPHANIE

Belfry's the bat's name she'd been wounded and couldn't fly but the woman kept her in a cage and took her to school for the kids to see to learn how not to hurt bats because in the day when Belfry sleeps the woman sees her foot move wing move and knows she's flying in her dreams don't we all baby don't we all Belfry you little bat.

Sam Doyle
house paint on tar and tin

His hands are wrapped in hornet's nests
his eyebrows launching from his face
BROWN BOMBER printed in gradeschool letters
behind his head
he loves his bulbous fists
his bare mouth smiling like a school boy z to sting.

A History of Languishes

In her introduction to *A Key into the Language of America*,
Rosemarie Waldrop speaks of the violent collage of phrases.

But instead of enacting the confrontation of the two cultures by
juxtaposition, often within a single sentence, Gweneth Rae wanted
to graft how the collision makes some biffy manifestations of
thought through the unfolding of language

    a) route of emigration
       by river (i.e. steamboat)/not land (i.e. wagon)
    b) the show up of a piece of old language (Cherokee)
    c) the journal of journey across _____
    d) other matters of interest that come to observation.

PRIMER OF THE OBSOLETE

Jut a word into the silence
hardly anyone notices
the corner room
a blue piece of wall
the sausage on a plate
as if looking for an airport.
It was not the same sound running over us
heard until we could not think.
My wife (meal maker for me) a-g(w')-s-ta'-yv-hv-s-gi'
cornbread a-l(i)-s-ta-i-di
sweet potatoes se'lu ga'-du
pumpkin pie nu:-n(a)-ni'nu-hi'd(a).
It was a wave sort.
A nothing at the rim.
A something at the core.
A switch from being watched.

For some the forced march intoward the country was enough to jump history like a keelboat over a puddle. It was not until the intrusion of other into the text we were the *invisibles* to them. Not knowing we have the sort from which they came. On the water it was done by them. Those boats moving along the river of the mantel. In a dream I was asleep. Hitting myself to wake. Stopped on the highway to make a left turn. The traffic passing on the shoulder.

I am your true woman, Blinky

No one has loved you like me
lets push through the halls
and rise over the house
pink as icing of the morning sun on a cupcake
the windows blow their openness to space
let's go baby let's toot out of here
that *lick of the lawn*
let's pilot our car with no place to land
we got mowed into the ages swell
the hosts take us to the limits of the driveway
the paper flying through the yard at dawn I got an idea
several of them really but one I'm zoned on
called me Blinky call me *zone*.

Tongues

You think of language as a formation which
does not ring a bill yet seems

a formidable field with birds.
If language follows a line,

the rev of engine before any take off,
you watch from behind a chain-link fence

you can almost get the toe of your shoe into,
but it slips sometimes

and you hold on with your fingers
and once you get over

you remember to speak about.
You hear yourself making a sound different

than when you heard your own voice.
The vent of language finding a point

turning in your mouth
a lock of birds exceeding.

CROWS

There were three crows in the morning grass wiping the underside
of their wings with dew. The back of their heads like Indian hair,
their shoulders holding out their feathers. You think at first they're
three dark spirits transformed by the wetness of light after their
night-shift. They're cleaning the coal dust and soot from their
wings still black at dawn. They wipe their bodies with their own
tongues they lick the fire out.

I Smelled Their Smoke

Over there on that hill
the shape-changers shifting,
the two-world walkers straggling,
hanging their feet over the dock of the next world.
They started little fires to dry their clothes
before heading into the dark.
They pulled their collars up around their necks,
shook out their trousers,
a little wag-tail tornado dipping from their fingers,
their boats for this world:
a little flame of leaves.

Oven dish

In a dream
she was in a pyrex dish in an oven
underwater
a bright yellow oven light
exciting the water
I was floating there
transparent as a jelly fish
with an umbilical cord
floating loose
you know you see in the water
all connected to the root.

The Great Spirit's Wife

He lead the way up a great ladder of small clouds,
and we followed him up through an opening in the
sky. He took us to the Great Spirit and his wife,
and . . . I saw they were dressed like Indians. Then he
showed us his hands and feet, and there were
wounds in them . . .

> Kicking Bear in a speech to
> a council of Sioux, 1890
> (from *Indian Oratory,* compiled
> by W. C. Vanderwerth, 1989)

She must be small
her ears made of spools
unwound from the thread
you know over the sundance ground
you saw white threads heading west
the hot afternoon you lay on the ground
in the shadow of the tent
looking skyward for the Great Spirit's wife
maybe she'd stop peeling potatoes long enough
to look down and spit on you
her mouth so pure and cool it would be like rain.

Photograph of the Ark

Here my father drove cattle to the ark.
His language obsolete as survival.
He sank into the unobserved
except the idea I have of him.
A camera not interesting in itself
but a tool I aimed high
leaving his head at the bottom of the photo.
Old Noah
the rain never stopped.

FLIPJACKS

How much more can be done?
The slate that was never clean
a pocket map
they are having
now retreats
didn't you always just hate them?
A sleeping bag on the floor
tracked with ashes
from the inevitable fire
the news of change so abrupt
into a world not known
not wanting to be known
but a duplicate
in the opposition of what calls.

THREE DEER

Three deer step from the woods.
They stand on the edge of the clearing.
Two female and one male with small, four-point horns.
They hold their bodies taut as they smell the air.
They have had lessons in danger.
They nudge the snow to find the field grass,
look quickly up.
They have long legs, slim as young girls
but a thickening body the legs can still carry
with the graceful awkwardness
of a junior high gym class.
One slips in the snow as she tries to hop back into the woods
but reappears
as we all do,
drawn to what we fear.

Ranger Otto Ranger Clive

"Well, Ranger Abbey," says Merle, "how do you
like it out here in the middle of nowhere?"

Desert Solitare
Edward Abbey

New wavers in the grass range. The radiant crew. Their mobiles
parked at the trusty curb. The Main Street patent office, land deed,
miner's co-op. The eager beaver caps. Don't they hear the lingo of
the past? A tango of moose antlers. Pie safe. Gun rack.

The flood then came of them on squatter ground. It was like this they said with their cross references they could plant the land. Their Bible was an act of faith by faith they believed their story was interesting. They gave us language we plastered with solecisms. Peavers. Padgers. They were much like words you could put your hand through though they were solid some of them anyway the known treaties a windsock. There were words yes they said was treaty (that could be broken if it suits). But no they insisted. We fried them with suspicion anyway. They had crossed the sea on dry ground compassed a wall until it fell down. Their references were intact. Abel offered a sacrifice. Enoch was translated and did not see death. Noah built an ark. Abraham left a place for another place dragged Isaac Jacob Joseph were the names they chosen. Then Moses. Joshua. The walls of Jericho. Rahab. Gideon Barak Samson David Solomon and his porcupines.

8 BALL

Just look how this *unoutstanding*
has such an aura about it
where life and death and glories
and ignominies of *infintessitude* pass.
I lift my head above the roof
and look at the mystery and majesty of the heavens.
The little smoking mound beneath it.
Polluted unfair suffering place.
God himself walked down to and was sent away
with bites in his hands and feet from the mongrel earth.
Black arrogant ball.
Willful baby.
The speck, blot, hubcap,
forgetful of the massive space it whines in
could squish it like a fly.
Little pike down the corridor of space.
This earth, this small fry.
We trust the little rolling marble.
This blue, this white streaked.
The long fall of it through space
more than an outpost yet not destination.
Heaven must be like, not tree, field, river,
but attitude, feeling, shape of relationship,
playing off one another,
the corners of thought in this little chickencoop.
Ancillary.
This something passing as a wagon train
to the outer limits of charted territory
to the whatsoever where all are bound.

Diane Glancy is a professor at Macalester College in St. Paul, Minnesota, where she teaches Native American literature and creative writing in poetry, fiction, nonfiction, and scriptwriting. Her recent books include the novels *The Mask Maker, Designs of the Night Sky*, and *Stone Heart: A Novel of Sacajawea* and a collection of plays, *American Gypsy*. Among her poetry collections are *The Relief of America, The Stones for a Pillow*, and *The Shadow's Horse*. A new collection of essays, *In-between Places*, is forthcoming. Glancy has received a National Endowment for the Arts Fellowship, the Minnesota and Oklahoma Book Awards, an American Book Award from the Before Columbus Foundation, and a Cherokee Medal of Honor from the Cherokee Honor Society in Tahlequah, Oklahoma. She earned her MFA from the University of Iowa.

THE
JUNIPER
PRIZE

This volume is the 29th recipient of the Juniper Prize
presented annually by the University of Massachusetts Press
for a volume of original poetry. The prize is named in honor
of Robert Francis (1901—1987), who lived for many years
at Fort Juniper, Amherst, Massachusetts.